Bobby Dean
and the Golden Egg

ALED JONES

Illustrated by Rosie Brooks

First published in Great Britain in 2022 by Hodder & Stoughton
An Hachette UK company

1

Copyright © Aled Jones, 2022
Illustrations © Rosie Brooks, 2022

A CIP catalogue record for this title is available from the British Library

Hardback ISBN 978 1 529 37616 6
eBook ISBN 978 1 529 37617 3

Typeset in Sabon MT by
Palimpsest Book Production Ltd, Falkirk, Stirlingshire

Printed and bound in Great Britain by Clays Ltd, Elcograf S.p.A.

Hodder & Stoughton policy is to use papers that are natural, renewable
and recyclable products and made from wood grown in sustainable forests.
The logging and manufacturing processes are expected to conform
to the environmental regulations of the country of origin.

Hodder & Stoughton Ltd
Carmelite House
50 Victoria Embankment
London EC4Y 0DZ

www.hodderchildrens.co.uk

Contents

1

Bobby's Back!

B obby Dean was swimming deeper and deeper
into the azure sea, a mighty whale leading him
towards the ocean floor. The creature's giant frame
sliced through the crystal-clear blue water, like a
mighty ocean liner carving its journey towards the
sun. As it guided Bobby downwards, the whale sang
Bobby a sea shanty. The notes formed clouds of tiny
air bubbles that tickled Bobby as he dived through
them.

> *Come swim with me, Bobby,*
> *in the wild, deep blue sea!*

To me, way hey, and blow the man down!
The ocean's my home, Bobby,
the best place to be!
To me, way hey, and blow the man down!

Ahead, the ocean's sandy floor stretched
out like the vast dunes of the Sahara
Desert. Bobby spied a perfectly round
coal-black pearl. He reached out to
pick it up.

'Ouch! Get off!'

Bobby woke up to see Noel, his pet mouse,
snuggled up under the warm fluffy ear of Ruffian,
Bobby's beloved dog. Noel was rubbing his nose.

'Sorry, Noel!' Bobby said. 'I was having an
amazing dream! I was diving with a
massive whale and we were
singing, and then I saw this black
pearl and I reached to pick it up!'

'Does my nose look like a black
pearl to you?' Noel asked.

2

Bobby laughed. 'A little bit,' he said.

Ruffian, Bobby's scruffy ginger dog and best friend, stretched out his back legs. With a little kick he dashed off the last remnants of sleep and licked Bobby's ear.

'Morning, Ruff!' Bobby said, ruffling the dog's furry head. Then, like he had done every morning since Christmas, he reached over to his snow globe on the windowsill and gave it a shake. As the snow cleared, images like movie clips flickered inside the globe.

'Look,' Bobby said to Noel, 'there's Dag!'

Dag was one of the dogs Bobby had met during his adventure on Scruff Island, only now Dag was out walking with his owner. He looks so happy, Bobby thought, waving at Dag, who barked back. The scene changed and Bobby saw the other dogs, Fly, Dink and Pip, all with their new owners and all so happy.

3

'Got any hotdogs going spare?' barked Pip.

Bobby gave the snow globe another shake to reveal a sunny beach. Sitting in a deck chair on the sand was a very large man with an enormous white beard that stretched all the way down to his tummy button. On his head was a straw hat to protect him from the sun.

'Hello, Santa!' said Bobby. 'How's the holiday?'

'Tickity-boo, Bobby!' Santa replied with a cheerful wave. 'You have a great day at school, now!'

As Santa reached for a very large and colourful drink, topped with numerous tiny umbrellas and skewers of fruit, Bobby shook the globe one last time. A moment later he saw Harold and his dad flying a huge multicoloured kite high in the air. Both were running and singing as the kite soared. Bobby gave them a wave.

'All present and correct!' said Bobby to Noel and Ruffian.

A shout bowled up the stairs to blast in through Bobby's bedroom door.

'Move it, Bobby! You don't want to be late on the first day of term!'

'Yes, Dad!' Bobby shouted back.

'Your mum's made you breakfast. And, for your convenience, she's put all of it in one enormous roll to take with you on the bus!'

Bobby ran to have a quick shower, then pulled on his uniform and headed downstairs into the kitchen. Ruffian was hot on his heels, Noel clinging onto the dog's neck like the tiniest jockey in the world.

'Smells amazing, Mum!' Bobby said, as she handed him a roll so big he could only just hold it with both hands. 'What's in it?'

'Everything is in it!' Bobby's dad laughed, throwing Ruffian a lovely, fat, juicy sausage.

Bobby's mum then counted off on her fingers the contents of his roll: 'There's bacon, sausage, beans, tomato, mushrooms, black pudding, white pudding, egg, a hash brown. Oh, and some haggis!'

Ever since Bobby could remember, his mum had fed him enormous meals and snacks in the hope he would grow as big as the other children his age, but Bobby had got used to being small and was quite happy just the way he was.

Bobby took a huge bite of the

roll as his mum gave Noel a pancake, who wrapped it around himself like a blanket.

'See you tonight!' Bobby shouted as he dashed from the house clasping his breakfast roll, his school bag flapping over his shoulder behind him. 'And thanks for breakfast!'

2

The Rich Man

Running along the lane, Bobby heard music in the air. He spotted the school bus winding its way towards him through the valley. At the end of the lane, parked in the road, was the largest, most expensive car Bobby had ever seen. It was a bright green Rolls Royce with wheels so shiny they made him squint if he looked at them. The car was surrounded by enormous bulldozers and huge trucks.

Bobby stared as the driver got out then walked to the end of the car and opened another door. A tall man, thin as a pine tree with no branches, climbed out. He was wearing a bright green suit and shoes as red as cherries.

The man waved at Bobby. 'I'm very rich, you know!' he shouted. 'Money is best!'

The man gave the driver a wad of money.

'Did you see that? I just gave my driver one thousand pounds! I bet you're really impressed, aren't you?'

Money didn't really interest Bobby. He knew that not having enough could make life hard. He also knew that having lots of it didn't necessarily make you happy.

'A thousand pounds for opening a door!' the man said. 'I could give you a thousand pounds right now, too, if I wanted. What do you think about that?'

Bobby gave a shrug, and said nothing.

'I'm so rich!' the man laughed, the sound thin and wrong, like the squeal of air being let out of a balloon. 'And being rich is best!'

Bobby took a bite of his
roll. Ruffian growled.

'That man is not nice at all,'
Noel said.

'Do you live here, boy?' the
man asked.

Bobby gave a nod. 'Why?'

'Hahaha! You're so poor!' the man
laughed, only this time the sound was that of the
dirtiest, grubbiest, rubbish-filled water, being sucked
down a disgusting, horrible drain. He pointed at
Bobby with a finger so thin it looked like a twiglet.
'And being poor like you is rubbish!'

Bobby was now feeling a little cross
with this rude man.

'Money isn't everything,' he said.

'Yes it is!' the man said, then he
removed something flat from a pocket
and started to open it. 'Do you
know what this is?'

Bobby stared. 'A map?'

'A map of this whole area,' the man said, then pointed at various things around them. 'Your horrible little house. That horrible little village up there. All these horrible fields and those horrible trees and that horrible stream. Horrible! I grew up here, you know? It was horrible.'

'It's not horrible, it's wonderful!' Bobby said.

The man ignored him and just kept speaking.

'I'm so rich I could buy all of it right now. This very minute! Maybe I will! Maybe I have! Because money is best!'

The man laughed again, folded up the map, and got back into his car. The window in the car door slipped down and he leaned his face out of it.

'I'm so rich I can do anything, and anything I do is always best because I'm so rich!'

The car drove off and the trucks and bulldozers followed on behind.

'Well, I hope we never see him again,' Noel said.

The school bus arrived and Bobby climbed aboard.

'Step on in, Bobby Dean!' said Legin, the driver. 'Your mates have saved you a seat at the back!'

Bobby thought about the horrible rich man, but then he saw his friends waving to him from the back of the bus.

'It's Easter term so time to learn!' Legin said. 'But on the way let the music play!'

He cranked up the tunes and the bus set off with a jolt.

'It's the boy with the golden chords!' shouted Doug as Bobby sat down.

'Where's Dash?' Bobby asked, seeing that the fastest girl in the school wasn't on the bus.

'Missed the bus on our first day back!' laughed Polo.

Tink held her nose.

'Means I'm stuck with all you stinky boys!' she said.

As the bus made its way to school, the gang talked about Christmas, what they'd done, and all the gifts they'd received. Polo had a new bike, Tink a telescope, and Doug a brand-new puppy called Star.

'At the moment he's just a tiny poop and wee machine!' Doug laughed. 'Cute, though. Loves a tummy rub and to chew your nose or ears!'

The bus came to a stop. Everyone stood up and shuffled to the door.

Legin shouted, 'Best you move faster, because look who's here, it's the best headmaster!'

The bus doors swished open and there was Mr Morris, the head teacher, his enormous frame filling the doorway.

'Good morning, Legin, and good morning everyone!' he said, his bellowing voice making the bus walls shake. 'Now, who can tell me, why did the one-eyed head teacher close down his school?'

Everyone groaned. Mr Morris had a reputation for telling the worst jokes.

'Please, sir,' Polo said. 'Don't—'

But it was already too late.

'Because he only had one pupil!' said Mr Morris, and shot out his arms ready for thunderous applause. 'Hahahahaha! I love jokes!'

No one laughed, not that Mr Morris seemed to mind at all.

'I won't be closing down this school though,' he said. 'Not a chance of it! Now, off you go to class!'

A while later, with registration done and everyone settled back into the normal school routine, Bobby was having a hard time with some difficult mathematics problems. Miss Evans, their teacher, was obviously trying to wake up their brains after the Christmas holiday. Bobby sat back in his seat and rubbed his eyes. He yawned, glancing out of the classroom window, then his eyes nearly popped out of his head. Racing across the fields towards school, he saw Ruffian, and on his back was Noel!

'It can't be!' Bobby muttered.

'Can't be what?' asked Tink.

'Nothing,' Bobby said.

'It can't be nothing?' Tink said. 'That doesn't make any sense at all, does it?'

Bobby opened his mouth to say something and was very pleased when the school bell rang. Grabbing his books and bag, he rushed out of the classroom and over to the school fence. Ruffian and Noel were on the other side.

'You can't be here!' Bobby said. 'School isn't for dogs and mice!'

Noel crossed his tiny arms. He stared defiantly at Bobby. Then he clicked his tiny fingers and grabbed Ruffian's ears as the dog jumped up onto his back legs and leant against the fence, putting Noel eye-to-eye with Bobby.

'It was Ruff!' Noel said. 'He's seen something! You need to listen to him. Now!'

Ruffian barked.

'But he's a dog!' Bobby said. 'And dogs don't speak. Not only that, I don't speak dog!'

Ruffian barked again.

'Yes, but I do,' said Noel. 'I tried to stop him coming here, but he just wouldn't listen! And I don't know if you've noticed, but I'm quite small, so stopping him wasn't really an option.'

'So, what is it, then?' Bobby asked. 'What is it that Ruff saw?'

Ruffian gave another bark and then a low rumbling growl.

'I'm telling him!' Noel said, tapping Ruffian on the nose. 'Don't be so impatient!'

Bobby laughed.

'It was something about a posh car,' said Noel. 'And a man dressed like a frog. Oh, and he was throwing his money about, I think!'

Ruffian barked and wagged his tail.

'He says he saw diggers and cranes and that he's worried something bad is about to happen!'

'How can anyone look like a frog?' Bobby asked. 'That doesn't make any sense at all!'

Ruffian gave his loudest bark yet.

'Dressed like a frog, not look like one,' said Noel. 'He was dressed in green.'

Then Bobby remembered the horrible rich man at the end of the lane. He was about to say something when a shout from behind caught his attention.

'Bobby Dean!'

Bobby turned from the fence to see Miss Evans staring at him.

'Break time finished a minute ago,' she said. 'You'll be late for assembly, and remember that Mr Morris is threatening that latecomers will have to do a handstand in front of the whole school. I'm sure you'd rather avoid that!'

'You'd best get going,' Bobby said to Ruffian and Noel, turning to run back into school. 'I'll see you later!'

'You can bet on it!' Noel said.

3

The Big News

Bobby was on a huge stage and standing in front
of an enormous crowd. Everyone was cheering
and shouting his name. A man in a top hat
approached him and handed him the biggest
chocolate egg he had ever seen.

'Bobby Dean is the winner!' the man bellowed.

The crowd cheered, 'Hurrah for Bobby Dean!
Hurrah! Hurrah! Hurrah!'

'Hurrah for me!' Bobby said, joining in. 'Hurrah! Hurrah! Hurrah!'

Something small and furry poked Bobby in the face.

'Ouch!'

'It's the middle of the night!' squeaked a small voice. 'Shush!'

Bobby opened his eyes. The first week of school had whizzed past faster than a hungry cheetah and he was very tired.

'I was having an amazing dream,' he said, but Noel was already back asleep and snoring.

Bobby lay in the darkness of his bedroom. Outside, a storm was throwing rain against the window. Wind was whipping through the trees, thin branches tapping on the roof of the house. Then Bobby heard the faint voices of his parents talking together somewhere in the house. He focused on their voices, blocking out all other sound.

'What about our house?' said his dad. 'And the farm? This is our home!'

'And the village, the school,' his mum replied.

They sounded worried, Bobby thought. But why?

'It won't happen,' his dad said. 'It can't.'

'But what if it does, Love?' his mum said. 'What then?'

Bobby really wanted to go downstairs to ask what they were talking about. But then he yawned and the yawn forced him to snuggle up under his duvet. And then he was asleep, dreaming of the weekend ahead.

Monday came around so quickly that Bobby could hardly remember what he had done at the weekend. There had been a lot of sitting around and yawning and very little else. Now, though, he was with his friends in assembly. Mr Morris was standing at the front wearing a huge pair of fluffy rabbit ears.

'I'm so egg-cited about this term!' he said. 'In fact, I'm hopping it's going to be egg-stra special!'

Mr Morris roared with laughter. Everyone else

groaned. Bobby, though, was too interested in the thing next to the head teacher and hidden under a white sheet.

Mr Morris clapped his hands loudly to get everyone's attention.

'First of all, the school trip. Anyone like to guess where we're going?'

'Back in time!' shouted a boy with ginger hair and a huge smile.

'Up Mount Everest!' said a girl with a freckled nose.

'Good suggestions, but no!' said Mr Morris. 'We're going to the zoo!'

Everyone cheered. Bobby loved zoos and punched the air with excitement.

'Thought you might like that,' Mr Morris said.

'Now, as we are coming up to Lent, can anyone tell me something lots of people do at this time of year?'

Doug put his hand in the air. 'Get a cold, sir!'

Everyone laughed.

'Give something up!' shouted Polo.

'Brilliant! Well done! So, what are we all giving up?'

The school erupted with everyone shouting out answers.

'Chocolate!'

'Falling asleep in class!'

'Pretending I'm a badger!'

'Telling bad jokes!'

'Farting and picking my nose!'

'I'm giving up haggis!' Mr Morris said. 'But what I haven't given up is coming up with wonderful ideas, and I had one last week. Do you want to know what it is?'

Everyone leaned forward, waiting for Mr Morris to deliver the news.

'Instead of giving something up for Lent, I want you all to take something up instead! What do you think?'

No one answered, not even Bobby.

'Let me explain,' Mr Morris said. 'I want everyone to do something good in our wonderful village. Help someone, for example, do their shopping, wash cars, pick up litter, sing songs, paint a fence! And here's the really exciting bit . . .'

The head teacher moved over to the large object and took hold of the sheet.

'The best idea of all wins this!'

With a dramatic flourish Mr Morris swooshed off the huge cloth. 'Ta-dah!'

Everyone gasped. There in front of them all was the most enormous golden egg Bobby had ever seen. It shimmered in the sunbeam as the children gathered round.

'Wow, it's so beautiful!'

'It looks like solid gold!'

'But it smells so good!'

'Can we touch it?'

'And just so you all know,' Mr Morris said, leaning forward as though letting them all in on a huge secret, 'it's made of chocolate!'

4

Coco D'Vine and the Giant Egg

M r Morris clapped his huge hands together once again.

'It gives me great pleasure to introduce to you the very person who made this massive and delicious and huge and scrummy and oooooh just look at all that lovely chocolate, so tasty, chocolate egg!'

Bobby was a bit confused by Mr Morris now, who was clearly rather overcome with excitement about the egg.

'Come in, Miss Coco D'Vine!'

Bobby stared as a tall woman walked onto the

stage. She was wearing a chocolate-brown boilersuit and a large belt hung with numerous whisks and spatulas and spoons. On her head was a chocolate-brown chef's hat that looked like a huge chocolate muffin. Pinned to her chest was a large badge which said, 'I LOVE CHOCOLATE'! Even her shoes were brown.

'Miss D'Vine grew up in the village,' explained Mr Morris. 'She is now one of the most famous chocolate makers in the world! Amazing!'

Everybody in the school assembly cheered, whistled and clapped.

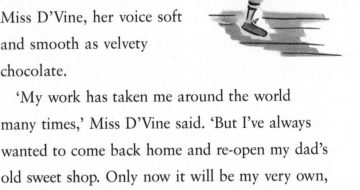

'You are so, so kind to welcome me to your school, you sweet, sweet lot!' said Miss D'Vine, her voice soft and smooth as velvety chocolate.

'My work has taken me around the world many times,' Miss D'Vine said. 'But I've always wanted to come back home and re-open my dad's old sweet shop. Only now it will be my very own, very special, and very, very delicious, chocolate shop!'

Bobby couldn't believe what he was hearing.

'A chocolate shop? Really?'

'Yes, really!' Miss D'Vine said. 'And there will be free hot chocolate for everyone!'

Everyone cheered once again, including Mr Morris and all of the teachers.

'This giant egg took a week to make,' Miss D'Vine explained. 'I made it to celebrate coming home to open my new shop. It's a very special egg and Mr Morris tells me you're all very special, too! So good luck! The winner is in for a very tasty treat! That's if they are strong enough to carry the egg home!'

'I'm strong enough!' said Polo, standing up and flexing his muscles.

Mr Morris stepped forward.

'Miss D'Vine is a very important person with very important people to see,' he said, 'so let's give her another round of applause as she leaves us today!'

Back in class everyone was talking all at once.

'That egg is mine,' Doug said. 'I'm going to raise money for a new playground by swimming a thousand lengths! No, a million!'

'I'm going to run a mile every day until the end of term,' said Sasha. 'I'm going to call it The Sasha

Dash and raise money for lots of fitness equipment for school!'

'I'm going to get people to guess how many hotdogs I can eat in an hour!' said Polo. 'I'm going to break the world record! Everyone will pay for a raffle ticket to guess the number I eat and the winner will get something amazing!'

'Like what?' asked Sasha.

Polo tapped the side of his head.

'That's a secret,' he said. 'But all the money I raise will go towards a new skate park! Yes!'

Polo punched the air as though he'd already won the egg.

Tink said, 'I'm going to set up a tech hospital where people can bring me their tablets and computers to fix.'

'Brilliant idea!' said Doug. 'What about you, Bobby?'

'How about I put on a big celebration concert on

the last day of term to show off
what everyone's done?' Bobby said.
'I'll call it an Egg-cellent
Egg-stravaganza!'

'What was that?'

Everyone turned at the booming voice to see
Mr Morris's head peeking round the classroom
door.

'It was Bobby,' said Doug.

Bobby waved at Mr Morris. 'My idea,' he said,
and explained it to the head teacher.

'Wonderful!' said Mr Morris. 'It's in the diary!
Hurrah!'

Then the head teacher disappeared and the door
slipped shut behind him.

'Looks like we're all sorted, then,' said Polo.

The gang all cheered.

The rest of the school day whizzed past and all
Bobby could really think about was the golden egg
and his idea, the Egg-cellent Egg-stravaganza. His
mind was buzzing and fizzing and popping with all
the things he could do, and he couldn't wait to get

home and tell his parents and Noel and Ruffian all about it.

When the day came to an end, Bobby raced to the bus, but as he came up to the school gate he saw on the other side of the road the posh car owned by the horrible man in the green suit. Towering over it, like quiet giants, were an enormous digger and an even more enormous bulldozer. Bobby saw that the car was empty. Then he spotted something else. Something furry. Something that should have been at home . . . He crossed over the road and quietly crept up behind the furry something and gave a loud cough.

The furry something jumped and turned round to stare at him. Bobby could now see that it was two furry somethings, the smallest of which looked rather cross.

'You're not supposed to be here!' said Bobby, staring at Noel. 'You should be at home!'

'We know that, but we're both really worried about the man in the green suit!'

'He's just rich and horrible, that's all,' said Bobby.

'But he's been sneaking around outside the school all day and taking photos!' said Noel. 'And he keeps pointing at the school and then laughing with the two drivers of the digger and the bulldozer!'

Ruffian barked.

'Oh, yes, I nearly forgot,' said Noel. 'We followed him around the village and he took even more photos!'

Bobby then remembered waking up in the night to hear his parents talking downstairs.

'I need to speak to Mr Morris,' Bobby said, and dashed back into school.

As he raced along to the head teacher's office, Bobby saw Mr Morris walking towards him. With him was the horrible man in the green suit.

43

'Hello, Bobby!' Mr Morris said. 'This is Mr D'Vine. He's a developer of new and amazing things and he has just given the school a large donation. I think we will use it for your end-of-term Egg-cellent Egg-stravaganza!'

Bobby didn't know what to say.

'Cat got your tongue?' Mr D'Vine said.

'You look worried,' Mr Morris said. 'If it's about the golden egg then there's nothing to fear, because I have everything protected by my fantastic haggis alarm system!'

Bobby wanted to say that he didn't trust Mr D'Vine, but Mr Morris was still talking.

'One wrong move,' the head teacher said, 'and a giant haggis comes out of nowhere and knocks the thief out – goodnight! It'll be offal for them!'

Mr Morris roared with laughter.

'Off you go, Bobby Dean, or you'll miss your bus!'

Outside, Bobby saw that Ruffian and Noel were no longer around. They must've gone home, he thought.

'Hurry up, Bobby, or we'll all be late!' Legin shouted from the school bus. 'Now get on the bus, mate, before they shut the school gate!'

When Bobby arrived home, his parents met him at the front door. They both looked worried.

'Ruffian has been missing all day!' they said.

'I'm sure he'll be back

45

soon,' Bobby said. 'He's probably just off having an adventure.'

He didn't want to tell them what Ruffian had really been up to with Noel. He was sure they just wouldn't believe him.

'You don't sound very worried,' Bobby's mum said.

'Ruffian can look after himself,' said Bobby. 'He's a very clever and very brave dog!'

And he's with a very special mouse friend, he thought. But that evening, when he went to bed, and Ruffian and Noel still weren't home, he couldn't help but be worried.

5

Ruff's Arrest

Bobby jolted awake, eyes wide open to thick darkness. He couldn't remember falling asleep. The only sound he could hear was his heart thumping hard in his chest. Then a creak sounded as his bedroom door opened.

'Bobby-Bean?'

Bobby switched on his bedside light.

'Mum?'

'It's Ruff,' his mum said.

Bobby jumped out of bed and ran

downstairs. He saw a flashing blue light outside.
In the kitchen, his dad was sitting with a police
officer.

'This is Officer Finch,' said Bobby's
dad.

'Have you found Ruffian?' Bobby
asked. 'Where is he? Is he
OK?'

Officer Finch asked,
'Can you describe your dog
for me, please?'

'He's big and scruffy and
cuddly,' Bobby said.

'And what colour is he?'

'He's a kind of ginger,' Bobby said. 'He's the best
dog ever.'

Officer Finch took out a photo from his jacket
pocket, looked at it, then handed it to Bobby.

'Is this your dog?'

'YES!' said Bobby. 'Where is he?'

'I'm afraid he is at the station,' said Officer Finch.
Bobby didn't understand.

'What? Why?'

'This morning, at approximately 2 a.m., this dog, your dog apparently, was found in the school.'

'Why? What happened?'

'The haggis alarm went off and we went to investigate,' said Officer Finch. 'It's a very good alarm, you know. A lot of haggis. We might build one at the police station.'

'What's that got to do with Ruff?' said Bobby, staring again at the photo of his best friend in the world.

'Your dog was covered in haggis and surrounded by the broken remains of a large golden chocolate egg,' Officer Finch said. 'Your dog will have to stay at the station overnight, and in the morning he will be fitted with an electronic tag so we can keep an eye on his whereabouts during our enquiries.'

Bobby didn't know what to say or do.

'I don't believe it,' he said, looking at his parents. 'Ruff is innocent! I know it!'

'We'll just have to sleep on it for now,' said his mum. 'In the morning, we can see what we can do.'

Police Officer Finch left the house and Bobby went back to bed. But as he lay down, he heard a faint tap-tap-tap at his window. Noel was on the other side of the glass covered in haggis and chocolate. Bobby opened the window and Noel fell into his bedroom.

'I've been hiding in that police car for hours!' Noel said.

Bobby found a small towel to clean Noel. 'What happened?' he asked.

'We were kidnapped is what happened!' Noel said. 'We were on our way home, like you told us to do, when a van pulled up, some men jumped out, and bundled Ruffian into a big sack! They didn't see me, on account of me being a mouse, but I just held on tight to Ruffian.'

'Where did they take you?' Bobby asked.

'The school hall!' said Noel.
'We were shaken out of the sack
and piled on the floor, then they
closed the door and locked us in.
We saw that the golden egg had
been smashed to pieces! Then the
alarm went off, Mr Morris's

haggis went everywhere, the police arrived, and
Ruff was arrested!'

Bobby looked at Noel,
who was wrapped up in the
towel. 'Mr D'Vine did this,'
he said. 'I don't know how or why,
but he did.'

'So, what are we going to
do about it?' Noel asked.

'Prove that Ruff is innocent!'
Bobby said. 'That's what!'

Very early the next morning, Dad drove them all to
the station to pick up Ruffian. Bobby had never

seen him so sad and the electronic tag looked very uncomfortable. Ruffian kept scratching and it would spin round his neck.

By the time Bobby walked into school, he could feel everyone staring at him. Word about the egg had got around quickly.

'You know Ruffian didn't do it, don't you?' he said to the gang at break time.

'Of course we do,' Doug said and patted Bobby on the shoulder.

Sasha gave Bobby a hug.

'We need to prove that Ruff is innocent,' Bobby said. 'I just don't know how.'

Tink stepped forward. 'We're here to help, remember?'

A loud voice burst from a speaker in the corner of the classroom. 'Bobby Dean to the head teacher's office! Immediately!'

In his office, Mr Morris was standing behind his desk with his hands on his hips. He looked bigger than ever.

'Now, before you say anything, Bobby, none of this is your fault. However, Ruffian is your dog and you must apologise to Miss D'Vine.'

'But Ruffian didn't do it,' Bobby said.

'He was found at the scene of the crime,' Mr Morris said.

'Yes, but Mr D'Vine—'

'No buts, Bobby,' Mr Morris said. 'You just

apologise and we must wait to hear from the police.'

That evening, Bobby's dad drove him to Miss D'Vine's house. Bobby knocked at the front door and waited, but there was no answer.

'Looks like there's no one in,' Bobby said, heading back to the car.

'We'll try again tomorrow, then,' his dad said, and they drove home.

At dinner, Bobby didn't feel very hungry. He watched Ruffian who was rubbing his neck and the electronic tag up and down the doorpost trying to remove it.

'You need to eat,' said his mum.

'I can't,' Bobby said. 'I'm too worried about Ruffian.'

'We all are,' said his dad. 'But there are other things to worry about.'

'What other things?' Bobby asked.

'It's the village,' said his dad.

'Not just the village either,' said his mum. 'The fields, the woods, our lovely farm!'

'I don't understand,' said Bobby.

'Neither do we,' said his dad. 'But a developer wants to change things round here. Build a theme park, would you believe! New houses, hotels. Awful.'

'But who would want to do that?' Bobby asked.

'Someone who cares only about money, is my guess,' said his dad.

'There's a meeting at the village hall this evening,' said Bobby's mum. 'We'll tell you more when we get back.'

Later that evening, Bobby was in his room with

Noel and Ruffian. Ruff was half asleep and scratching at his tag, and so grumpy he'd flopped in the corner. Bobby knew it was best just to leave him.

'This all sounds very serious,' Noel said.

'It's Mr D'Vine,' Bobby said. 'I just know it! He set Ruffian up because he knows we are on to him.'

'My small mousey brain doesn't understand,' Noel said.

But Bobby wasn't listening. He was singing. And as the music flowed from him, Noel quickly jumped into his pocket. Then Bobby felt a familiar tingling in his toes and heard the sound of running water and flutes. He closed his eyes as he shot through the galaxy with the stars pointing him on his way to an exciting new adventure!

6

Back in Time

Bobby opened his eyes to find himself flying towards a huge pulsing blob of bright, swirling colours. It looked like a rainbow in a blender! He was going so fast that his ears popped. Then he heard a high-pitched 'zip' sound, the colours swallowed him up, and then everything was silent.

'Snow!' Bobby said.

Wherever they were, a thick blanket of snow was falling. It was like someone had emptied the world's largest sack of feathers from the sky.

'Good job I'm wearing this coat,' said Noel as he crawled out of Bobby's pocket.

Bobby stared down at Noel. He was wearing a black top hat and a black coat that stretched down to his knees. On his feet he had tiny little black boots, and wrapped around his neck was a flowery silk scarf. Bobby realised then that he was dressed just the same, even down to the scarf.

A shout made Bobby jump as a man whizzed past on a wooden bike. No sooner had he gone when Bobby then had to dodge out of the way of a horse and carriage. Wherever Bobby looked, people and horses and carts and strange wooden bicycles were rushing past. But there were no cars, he noticed.

Bobby sucked in a deep

breath and his nostrils were filled with icy air and
the sweet smell of roasting chestnuts. Across the
road he saw a lady huddled
around a small fire
trying to keep warm.
Next to her stood an
old man with a beard
almost down to his
waist, dressed in rags
and playing a penny
whistle, an empty cap

placed on the ground in front of him. A woman
walked past and tossed a coin into the hat.

'It's like we've landed in a scene from an old
Christmas card!' said Bobby.

Another shout made Bobby jump.

'Look out!'

Then Bobby felt himself being yanked backwards
as a huge cart drawn by a big black horse whooshed
past, its hooves the sound of thunder against the
cobbled street.

Bobby and Noel turned around to see who had saved their lives. Standing there in front of them was a girl who looked the same age as Bobby.

'That was too close,' said Bobby.

'You saved our lives!' said Noel with a bow. 'Thank you.'

'You're a mouse,' the girl said.

'I am indeed,' said Noel. 'And the most finest of mouses you will ever meet!'

The girl laughed.

'This is Noel,' said Bobby. 'My name is Bobby.'

'Florence,' the girl said, shivering, and wrapping her arms

around herself against the chill wind blowing down the street.

Bobby noticed then how pale and thin Florence seemed. Her clothes were worn and full of holes. 'You look cold,' he said.

'I'm freezing,' Florence said.

'Then you should get home,' said Bobby.

'Don't have a home,' said Florence. 'Or parents. It's just me and my brother and a few others.'

Bobby was about to say something when a shout cut across from the other side of the street.

'Look, there's fleabag Florence!'

Bobby looked over to see a plump boy with red cheeks dressed head to toe in very expensive, very warm clothes. He looked like he could burst at any moment. He was standing with a small group of children.

'Florence fart breath!' shouted a blonde girl wearing a huge furry hat and fur coat.

Another boy stepped forward, skinny as a toothpick and pale as the snow he was standing in.

'Where did you get your clothes from?' he teased Florence. 'The dustbin?'

Then he threw a snowball and ran off, the rest of the children following on behind.

Bobby turned to say something to Florence only to find that she had vanished.

'Where did she go?'

'Look!' Noel said, pointing at footprints in the snow.

'Come on, then,' Bobby said, and started to follow them.

Snow and ice glittered and shone on the cobbled road in front of them as they followed Florence's hurried steps to a tumbledown house. Slates were missing from the roof, the windows were boarded up and the front door was rotting and crumbling to nothing.

An elderly gentleman came shuffling past, dragged along by a dog on the end of a leash.

'Excuse me,' Bobby said. 'But what year is this?'

'I beg your pardon?' the man replied. 'Has the cold made me deaf or did you ask what year it is?'

'I did,' said Bobby.

'Why, it's 1884, of course!' said the man. 'Victorian London at its coldest!'

And off he went, slipping in the snow as the dog pulled him along.

'Wow!' Bobby said. 'We've travelled back in time. How cool is that, Noel?'

Noel gave a shiver. 'Cool? It's freezing is what it is!' he said.

'Do you think Florence is in there?' Bobby shivered, looking at the house in front of them.

'Only one way to find out,' said Noel.

Bobby and Noel squeezed through the door and into a hallway so cold their breath turned to thick icy clouds in the air. Exploring the house, they came into a large gloomy room that smelled of damp and candle wax. Huddled together under old clothes and blankets were a group of children warming their hands on a lit candle.

'Florence!' Bobby said. Florence was sitting next to a boy who was curled up on a mound of rags and covered in dusty blankets and old jackets.

'You followed me?' Florence replied. 'Why?'

'We were worried,' Bobby said. 'Those children were horrible.'

'We're used to it,' Florence said, resting a hand on the boy beside her. 'I had to rush off, you see. It's Tom, my brother. He's ill. I can't leave him for long.'

'Why don't you take him to the doctor?' asked Bobby.

'A doctor?' said a boy around the candle. 'You having a laugh? Doctors cost money. And we ain't got none!'

'Cleaning chimneys and muck from the horses don't make us millionaires!' said a girl.

70

'But what about food?' Noel asked.

'Crikey, a talking mouse!' said another boy. 'You weren't going crazy then, Flo!'

'Told you!' Flo laughed.

'We share what we have,' a girl said and offered Bobby a crust of bread. 'It's all we've got.'

Bobby looked at Noel. 'We have to help them,' he said.

'I hear you, boss,' Noel said. 'Any ideas?'

'Not yet,' said Bobby. 'But it won't be long, I'm sure of it!'

'And so am I, Bobby my boy,' Noel said. 'So am I!'

The next day Bobby and Noel joined the group as they did what they could to make some money.

'You weren't joking when you said it was mucky business!' said Bobby as he shovelled hot horse poop from behind a carriage into a big sack.

When the sack was full, Bobby went with Florence to a beautiful big house on a quiet street. The door was opened by a tall woman with a mean face. She was wearing a very expensive dress of purple and gold. Behind her Bobby could see a party. Everyone was laughing and eating and drinking and playing games. And there in the middle of it all was the plump boy in expensive clothes. He walked over to join the woman at the front door.

'It's the stinky poop people, Mummy!' the boy said.

'Tarquin, darling, be an angel and pay them.'

The boy threw some money at Florence's feet then slammed the door.

Back at the derelict house Florence went to check on her brother. He was pale and wouldn't wake up

when they tried to shake him. His skin was clammy
and as white as wax.

'We don't have enough money to make him
better,' Florence said. 'I don't know what to do!'

Bobby watched as Florence ran out of the freezing
living room in floods of tears. Then he remembered
the man with the penny whistle.

'You have an idea, don't you?' Noel said.

Bobby grinned. The best idea ever!' he said.

7

Tarquin and the Sticky Fudge

Bobby Dean was woken up by the sound of his teeth chattering. Outside, the wind was a howling wolf forcing its way through the broken windows, a sharp-tongued phantom blasting its icy breath into the living room.

After a breakfast of stale bread and a shared jug of water from melted snow, Bobby gathered everyone together to explain his plan.

'We're going to do some busking,' he said.

'We're street kids!' said Florence. 'We can't sing!'

'Anyone can sing,' Bobby said.

Bobby could tell from the looks on everyone's faces that no one believed him.

'We're going to sing one of my favourite songs,' he said, remembering his dream about the whale. 'It's a sea shanty!'

'But we're nowhere near the sea!' said Florence.

'Trust me,' Bobby said. 'Now, this is how it goes . . . *Come swim with me, children, in the wild, deep blue sea! To me, way hey, and blow the man down*!'

Rehearsal over, and once again out on the cold street, Bobby placed a hat on the ground to collect money.

'Now, remember everything I taught you,' he said. 'You can all sing!'

Bobby counted everyone in.

At first no one sung, then Florence gave a cough, opened her mouth, and out her voice came. Soon, the others followed, their voices twisting and turning together, looping and dancing in the falling snow.

'Brilliant!' Bobby said. 'That's it! Perfect! What did I tell you?'

They kept on singing and soon a
small crowd had gathered around.

'Look at the hat!' Noel said.

The hat was overflowing with
coins.

'Encore! Encore!' shouted the small crowd. 'We
want more!'

Then another voice joined in.

'Yuck, it's foul Florence and her stinky friends!'

Bobby saw the plump boy,
Tarquin, in the crowd.

'Ignore him!' he said.
'Keep singing! You're
amazing!'

'I'll sing for you,'
shouted Tarquin.

'Florence is a stinker, and
her breath reeks of poop! If
you give her money, then you stink like gloop!'

Tarquin laughed and Bobby watched as the
boy popped a large lump of sticky fudge into his
chubby face.

'I'd give you some,' Tarquin said, 'but you're too poor and smelly for delicious sweets!'

Then, just as he went to pop another piece of fudge into his mouth, a lump of snow fell off the roof of a house behind the crowd and landed on his head.

Everyone laughed.

Tarquin went to say something, his face red, but when he opened his mouth, no sound came out.

'Not so funny now, is it?' Florence said.

Tarquin grabbed his throat and his face grew even redder.

'Something's wrong,' Bobby said.

'He's choking!' Noel squeaked.

Florence rushed over to Tarquin. She whacked him on the back with all her might. Tarquin staggered forward but continued to get redder and redder. Florence hit him again.

'What are you doing?' cried Bobby.

'Quick, he's got a piece of fudge stuck in his airway. He can't breathe!'

Florence hit him again and the boy flopped into the snow waving his arms in panic.

'Bobby! I need to borrow your mouse!'

'I have a name,' Noel said as Florence grabbed him by the tail. 'Hey! Get off!'

Florence held Noel in one hand and a big clump of Tarquin's hair in the other. She yanked his head back and the boy knelt hopelessly in the snow, his mouth gaping open.

Before Bobby could stop her, Florence dangled Noel over Tarquin's mouth. 'Can you see it?' she asked.

'See what?' Noel said.

'The fudge! He's choking on it!' Florence replied. 'We need to fish it back out! Quickly!'

Noel looked down into the boy's throat.

'Yes, I can,' he said. 'And it's very disgusting!'

Florence lowered Noel into Tarquin's mouth.

'Got it!' Noel shouted.

Florence yanked Noel back out into the open air.

Tarquin was on his hands and knees panting for breath. 'Why did you save me?' he spluttered.

'Because I treat everyone the same,' Florence said. 'Even if they are a bit rotten.'

Tarquin stood up. 'I'm so sorry,' he said. 'How can I thank you?'

'What we need is a doctor,' Florence said. 'And you don't look old enough.'

'I'm not,' Tarquin said. 'But my father is. Are you ill?'

'Not me, my brother,' Florence said. 'Will he help?'

'Yes,' Tarquin said. 'Come on!'

Back at the derelict house, Bobby and Noel sat with Florence as Tarquin's father closely examined Tim, her brother.

'I'm glad we found you when we did. It's surprising how quickly things can become serious – your actions have saved this little boy's life. With a small amount of this medicine he's going to be fine,' said Tarquin's father. 'But to recover well, good food and lots of rest is what he needs. And somewhere warm to do it in. And the same goes for the rest of you.'

'But we live here,' Florence said. 'This is all we have.'

'Not anymore,' said Tarquin's father. 'After what you did today for my Tarquin, you're all coming back with us.'

That night all the rich and poor children sat together in front of a crackling log fire, laughing and joking with one another. Florence had her little brother in a deep embrace. Bobby conducted everyone in a new song which they performed for Tarquin's mum and dad. And then Bobby's feet started to tingle. And as suddenly as they had arrived in Victorian London they were once again zipping back home through the swirl of multicolours.

8

A New Member of the Gang

With the Egg-cellent Egg-stravaganza and the worries about Ruffian and Mr D'Vine, Bobby forgot all about his Victorian adventure until Tuesday the following week. As Mr Morris started assembly he was joined at the front of the hall by a new pupil.

'I want you all to welcome our newest pupil, and Miss D'Vine's daughter,' Mr Morris boomed. 'Flo!'

'Bet she has chocolate for breakfast, lucky thing!' said Polo. 'Then hotdogs for lunch with chocolate sauce! Delish!'

'She looks really nice and friendly, don't you think?' said Sasha.

The girl reminded Bobby of Florence from his adventure in Victorian London. He knew it couldn't be the same girl, but it was still a little strange.

The head teacher's voice boomed out once again. 'Bobby Dean! I want you and your friends to show Flo around the school and make sure she's looked after.'

In class, the gang asked Flo lots of questions.

'So, do you get chocolate for every meal of the day or just breakfast?' asked Polo.

'I actually do!' Flo said.

'Where were you at school before here?' asked Tink.

'I haven't been to school for ages, actually,' said Flo. 'I wasn't very well for a long time but now I'm much better.'

'Great news!' said Sasha, ''cos now you're part of our gang!'

'Sounds fun!' said Flo.

'I came round your house last night to say sorry to your mum about the egg,' Bobby said.

'Did you?' Flo said. 'She was picking me up from the hospital. Anyway, she doesn't believe it was your dog.'

'Really? Why?' Bobby asked.

'Because she thinks it was her horrible jealous brother, that's why,' said Flo, spitting out her words. 'He's a nasty bully and he's followed us here!'

The gang looked at each other, not sure how to react.

'Why has he followed you?' asked Doug.

'He wants to smash up the town and build something horrible in its place.' she said. 'All because he thinks that my grandad's shop should be his, because he's older. But it was Mum who helped Grandad in the shop all those years ago. He didn't do anything. Not ever!'

'Who is he?' asked Sasha.

'You mean you haven't seen him driving around in his flashy car and wearing that revolting green suit?'

Bobby gasped. 'Your uncle is Mr D'Vine?'

Flo gave a nod.

'Then you know what this means, don't you?' Bobby said, looking at the gang.

'Sure do,' said Polo.

'What?' Flo asked.

Sasha grinned. 'We're going to stop him!'

That evening after dinner, Bobby and the gang were meeting in their den.

'All those in favour of Flo officially being in the gang say "hotdogs"!' said Polo.

'Hotdogs!' everyone replied.

'Thanks so much,' said Flo, reaching into her pocket. 'This is the best day ever!'

'How's everyone doing with taking something up for Lent?' Sasha asked.

'I've run so many miles now that I've lost count!'

'Running is easy,' Doug said. 'Swimming is so hard! There's so much to remember, like how to kick, how to use your arms, how to breathe!'

'You don't know how to breathe?' Bobby said. 'But you'll drown!'

'Well, I'm practising my hotdog eating, that's for sure,' said Polo and tapped his tummy. 'What about you, Tink?'

Tink said, 'I've put an advert up in a local shop. You'd be amazed how many people don't know how to use their computer properly.'

Bobby said, 'I've not really thought about the egg-stravaganza. Any ideas?'

'We'll need lots of balloons,' said Sasha.

'And music,' said Tink.

Doug said, 'We should have a parade!'

'With lots and lots of food!' added Polo.

Flo laughed and said, 'I have someone else I want you to meet.'

Standing proud and small on the palm of Flo's hand was a mouse.

'This is Nippy!'

'She's adorable!' said Sasha.

'Amazing!' said Tink.

'I must introduce her to my dog,' said Doug, 'although that might not be the best idea!'

As everyone fussed around Nippy and Flo, Bobby noticed another little mouse staring in from the windowsill.

'By the way, in assembly earlier I noticed that your voice is really . . . amazing!' said Bobby, and then instantly he felt a bit awkward – he was so used to other people telling him how amazing HIS voice was, it felt strange being the one to notice someone else's.

'I love to sing! It's the coolest thing! And it's always been my family's thing since my great-great-great-aunt! She was an orphan and sang in a street choir for money! Now that's cool!' She took a deep breath and added, 'Apparently she saved a boy's life.'

'Wow!' said Bobby, 'I wish I'd met her!'

And there in that moment Bobby was transported back to Victorian London. The memory made him smile.

'Apparently I'm just like her!' said Flo.

That night in bed as Bobby was struggling to keep his eyes open, the last words he heard were from Noel.

'Wow, another mouse in the gang. I'm not sure whether I'm happy or sad about that . . . I hope she's nice. How do you feel about another singer, Bobby?'

'I think I'm excited about the extra fun it will bring. I hope you can feel the same too, Noel?'

Ruffian's collar let out another clatter as the dog spun it round for the thousandth time.

'Don't worry, Ruffian. Now we know more about Mr D'Vine I'm sure we'll prove your innocence soon,' said Bobby.

And with that they all drifted off to sleep.

9

A Trip to the Zoo

The trip to the zoo promised by Mr Morris at the start of term arrived quickly.

'Don't forget these!' said Bobby's mum, rushing out of the kitchen with three huge tins full of cupcakes.

'Your mum's made enough for the hippos and the elephants too!' laughed Bobby's dad.

'And I've packed you a picnic in your backpack too,' said his mum. 'Hope it's not too heavy!'

Bobby could hardly see over the top tin as he slowly made his way down the lane. He heard the singing before he saw Legin's bus.

> *Jump on board Two by Two,*
> *'Cos we're going to the Zoo!*

> *We might see a cuckoo or a kangagoo,*
> *Repeat after me . . .*
> *Yahoo! Yahoo!*

Legin opened the doors and peered over his green shades. 'We're going to the zoo! You can come too! Especially if you have food! Drop the tins with me and sit yourself down!'

Miss Evans smiled at Bobby from a seat at the front of the bus, where she was sitting with Mr Morris. 'Are you sure

you've brought enough food?' she asked, checking
Bobby off on the register.

Bobby made his way to the back of the bus,
where he noticed that even Sasha had made it on
time. He lifted up his packed lunch to show
everyone.

'I've got three scotch eggs, a homemade pork pie
bigger than my head, dozens of sandwiches, a bag
of apples, chocolate, biscuits, cake . . .'

'All I've got is a cheese and pickle sandwich!' said
Tink, 'So you'll be sharing your feast with me!'

Bobby continued digging into his bag and bringing out food. 'Ten drumsticks, cheese and biscuits, oh, and a juice! And lots of crumbs!'

'So basically enough for us and the entire zoo!' said Sasha. 'I'm so excited to get there!'

'If Bobby eats all his lunch he'll be bigger than the zoo's giant rabbit,' said Doug. 'Apparently it's bigger than me! I read about it in the local paper.'

'Must be true, then,' Bobby laughed.

'This is my first ever school trip,' said Flo.

'I can't wait to see the crocodiles!' said Polo.

'Snap out of it!' said Sasha.

As the bus made its way out of the village, Bobby saw something strange in a large field. 'Look!' he said, pointing through the window.

The field was filled with construction vehicles. There were cranes, diggers, skips and people in bright yellow vests.

'Whatever it is they're doing, we have to stop it,' Bobby said.

'But how?' asked Flo.

Bobby wasn't sure, but that didn't mean he was going to do nothing. He just needed time to think.

When the bus finally arrived at the zoo, Legin opened the doors.

Everyone rushed off the bus.

'First stop the giant rabbit!' shouted Doug.

'After we get an ice cream!' suggested Bobby.

'And maybe a hotdog!' said Polo.

The gang ran from
one section of the
zoo to another
taking in all the
different animals.

'Woah! Look at
the size of that
poop!' Polo said,

pointing to where two elephants were being hosed
down by their keepers.

'And it stinks!' shouted Sasha, putting a hand to
her nose.

'Well, big elephant, big poop!' said Flo. 'And that
one's massive!'

Bobby's mind wandered back to
Victorian London and his time
with Flo's great-great-great-aunt.
Horse poop was bad enough.

A small voice interrupted Bobby's thoughts. 'That
pong is so bad my nose might drop off!'

Bobby opened his bag to see Noel staring at him,
a tiny paw holding his nose.

'You're meant to be home with Ruff!'

'I slept in your bag last night to get away from
your snoring,' said Noel. 'Didn't wake up until that
horrible stink!'

'Snoring! You were talking in your sleep,' joked
Bobby.

Some time later, having spent a
good amount of time with the
penguins, Bobby and the gang
were staring at the giraffes.

'Look!' said Sasha. 'Over there!'

The gang turned to see Mr D'Vine
in his green suit. He was speaking loudly
into a gold mobile phone.

'What's he doing here?' Bobby asked.

'Never mind him,' said Tink. 'Look at those two boys!'

At the other side of the giraffe enclosure, Bobby saw two boys throwing sweets at the giraffes. They were laughing and dancing around as though what they were doing was the best thing ever.

'Oh no!' said Flo.

'What's up?' Bobby asked.

'They're my little cousins,' Flo said. 'They're horrible!'

'A thousand pounds if you hit him on the head!' said Mr D'Vine, handing the boys even more sweets.

Bobby knew he had to do something, but before he could, the boys had run off.

'My uncle is a rotten pig!' said Flo.

'And that's being nasty to pigs!' Sasha said.

Bobby saw the glint of the golden mobile phone

and that the man was still deep in conversation, so he crept closer to see if he could hear what he was talking about.

'Who cares about stupid animals anyway?' Mr D'Vine said, his voice thin and raspy like wind through a comb. 'And zoos are so boring and a waste of time! Let's see if we can knock the whole thing down and build a massive concrete storage unit and charge £20 a day for people to store things they don't use! Now that would be smashing!'

Bobby felt Flo grab his arm.

'He's here to try and destroy everything!' she said. 'And I don't know if we will be able to stop him!'

10

The Giant Rabbit

'Hey, where have all the snakes gone?' Polo had his face pressed up against the glass cabinet where a python was supposed to be.

'No snakes anywhere?' Sasha asked.

Bobby heard some banging nearby. 'Look,' he said, pointing. 'They've scared them off!'

Everyone looked to see the two horrible boys thumping every display cabinet as they ran around laughing.

'They've scared off all the snakes!' said Polo and stared at the two boys. 'Oi! You! Shove off!'

Bobby was impressed with Polo's bravery.

The two boys looked back at the gang. 'Yeah? And what are you going to do about it?'

Before anyone could answer, they ran away.

'Come on, let's go somewhere else,' Bobby said.

A few minutes later, and with the two boys no longer in sight, Bobby and the others stopped to look at a huge African elephant who was lazily chewing through a ball of hay.

'That trunk is massive!' said Sasha.

'Just imagine how many hotdogs you could hoover up with that!' laughed Polo.

'So, what animal do you reckon you'd be?' asked Tink. 'I reckon I'd be a panther! What about you, Dash?'

'A cheetah,' Sasha said. 'Fastest animal on the planet!'

'Except for the peregrine falcon,' said Doug.

'Yes, but that's a bird,' Sasha said.

'I reckon Bobby would be a bear because he's ace at building dens,' said Polo.

'And I'm the gorilla!' Doug said, and beat his chest, jumping from foot to foot.

'How about you, Flo?' asked Bobby.

'A lioness,' Flo said. 'Strong, like my great-great-great-aunt, and with huge teeth to scare off my uncle and his two terrible sons!' She lifted her hands in front of her and made them into claws. 'Rrrrrrrrrooooooaaaarrr!'

RrrroOOOaaarrr!!!

Running away from Flo in mock terror, the gang found themselves in front of an enclosure. Inside it was the largest rabbit any of them had ever seen.

'I told you he was massive!' said Doug.

A sign on the door read: *'This is a Flemish Giant Rabbit. He's a little*

excitable so please don't make loud noises and keep
your distance as his behaviour can be a little
unpredictable'.

A thunderous crack made everyone jump.

'What was that?' Bobby said, then he saw the two
boys falling from a tree near to the rabbit enclosure.
They got to their feet, brushed themselves down
and walked over to the rabbit.

'Ha, a stupid rabbit!'

'Yeah, let's poke it with a stick!'

Taking a branch snapped from the tree, they
shoved it through the enclosure to prod the giant
rabbit. The creature jumped and ran off to
hide.

'Ha! Run rabbit! Run! Run! Run!'

Tink
walked
over to the
two boys.
'Stop that!
Right now!'

'We can do what we want!' the boys said. 'Know why? Because we're rich and being rich is best!'

They stuck the stick in once again and tried to find the rabbit.

Bobby had seen enough and stepped in front of the boys. He grabbed the stick and threw it away.

'Hey, who do you think you are?' said the boys.

'Someone who's going to stop you, that's who,' Bobby said, but before he could say anything else, he started to sing.

Then his toes tingled and he heard
the sound of running water and
sweetly singing flutes, and before he
could do anything to stop it he
was whizzing through the stars!

11

Sir Hopsalot

Bobby saw that he was on a surfboard of tiny stars. They were guiding him through the galaxy, riding huge waves of asteroids and shooting stars. Noel looked up at Bobby from a coat pocket.

'Want to go faster?' shouted Bobby.

'Yes!' Noel said.

Bobby pushed down harder with his feet and pointed forward with his finger and the star surfboard hurled itself forwards.

As they approached the multicoloured blob, Bobby and Noel closed their eyes. Then . . . silence!

'You ready for another adventure, Bobby?' whispered Noel.

'You bet!' answered Bobby, and slowly opened his eyes to the brightest, most vividly coloured landscape he had ever seen.

'I wish I had sunglasses!' said Noel.

Everywhere Bobby looked the world shone and danced with colour. The sun, as yellow as the brightest, freshest of egg yolks, seemed to bathe the world below in glittering gold. He saw trees and fields so

green they looked like they had just been freshly
painted. A river bubbled past, the water clear as
crystal, dashing itself on rocks to explode into
diamonds. He saw flowers and fruit, birds and all
kinds of creatures everywhere, their colours
reminding him of something.

'A cartoon!' Bobby said. 'That's what this looks
like!'

Bobby walked down to the river and scooped up
some of the water in his hand for a drink.

'Wow!' he said. 'Noel, you have to try this! It's
cold and sweet and totally amazing!'

Noel dipped his snout into the
water, but as he did so a shout
broke the moment.

'Please help me!'

'Why, what's up?' Noel asked,
looking at Bobby.

'That wasn't me,' Bobby said.

The shout came again.

'It's coming from behind those bushes!' said
Noel.

Bobby crawled on all fours through the bush,
Noel on his back. Pushing through the other side he
found himself in front of a brown rabbit. It was
dressed like a knight, with a chainmail shirt and
leather trousers. The rabbit's back leg was caught
in a trap and it was using its sword to try to free
itself.

'Ah, good Sir Bobby!' the rabbit
said. 'I need your help! Quick!'

'You know who I am?'
Bobby said.

'Of course!' the rabbit
said. 'You are Sir Bobby!
The bravest boy in all the
land! And you are here to help me! Hurrah!'

Bobby said, 'I need to get you out of that
trap.'

'Indeed you do, and most swiftly!' the rabbit said.
'Use that stick over there.'

Bobby looked to see where the rabbit was

pointing, grabbed the stick, then prised apart the trap's jaws.

The rabbit jumped free from the trap.

'Hurrah!' the rabbit said. 'Sir Hopsalot is free once again to save the kingdom with the mighty Sir Bobby at his side!'

'Why does the kingdom need saving?' Bobby asked.

'Why, because of Wizard Greesgate!' Sir Hopsalot said. 'He is the most evil and foul wizard in all the world. He's imprisoned King Colin and his daughter Anne, made everyone very unhappy and,

worst of all, forced everyone to eat eggs for
breakfast!'

'What's wrong with eggs?' Noel asked.

'You try eating them every day for weeks on end,'
said Sir Hopsalot. 'It gets very smelly, I can tell you!
Such a horrible pong!'

'This wizard sounds awful,' said Bobby.

'I was trying to rescue the princess when I got caught in this trap,' said Sir Hopsalot. 'Wizard Greesgate has set traps all over the kingdom. And guess what he does to anyone he catches?'

'Puts them in prison?' Bobby asked.

'He turns them into chocolate!'

'Why has he taken the king and the princess as prisoners?' Noel asked.

'He's working on a spell to make the princess fall in love with him,' Sir Hopsalot said. 'Then he'll marry her and rule forever! This cannot be so! I shall not allow it! Well, I won't if you help me, that is.'

Bobby looked at Noel. 'Best we help Sir Hopsalot,' he said.

'I think that's why we're here,' Noel said.

'Hurrah!' Sir Hopsalot cheered. 'Now follow me!'

'Where to?'

'Why, to the Forest of No Return! Onwards!'

'That doesn't sound very inviting,' Bobby said.

'It isn't,' Sir Hopsalot said. 'It's terrifying! Come on! Follow me!'

And before Bobby or Noel could say anything else, the rabbit knight bounded off and they raced after him.

12

The Golden Egg

'Wow, now that's a castle!' Noel said.

Bobby, Noel and Sir Hopsalot were hiding in a bush staring up at the castle. Bobby was amazed at all the turrets and towers. This was a fairytale castle, with shiny white walls and flags on every pinnacle.

'Where's the princess?' Bobby asked.

'She's in that well over there,' Sir Hopsalot said.

Bobby saw the well in front of the castle. Two

soldiers were guarding it. 'What are we going to do about them?' he asked.

'Leave that to me!' Sir Hopsalot said. Then he hopped out into the open and shouted, 'Good day, you horrible soldiers!'

The two soldiers turned to stare at Sir Hopsalot just in time to see two carrots flying through the air to bonk them on their heads. They both dropped to the ground and then Bobby heard them snoring.

'You knocked them out with carrots?' Bobby said.

'Of course!' said Sir Hopsalot. 'Carrots help you see in the dark, remember?'

Bobby was confused. 'What's that got to do with using them to knock people out?'

'I've no idea!' Sir Hopsalot laughed. 'Now, to rescue the princess!'

At the well, Bobby shouted down into the darkness, 'My name is Bobby Dean and we're here to rescue you!'

'We?' the princess replied from below.

'Yes, me, Noel and Sir Hopsalot,' Bobby said.

'Nigel's here as well?' the princess asked.

'Nigel? Who's Nigel?' said Noel, then looked at the rabbit knight. 'Your first name is Nigel?'

'Of course!' Sir Hopsalot said. 'And a strong, wondrous name it is too, don't you think?'

'Well then, Sir Nigel Hopsalot,' Bobby said, 'how are we going to rescue the princess?'

'With a magic egg, of course!' Sir Hopsalot said. 'Tell them about the egg, your princessness, before it's too late!'

'Too late for what?' Noel asked.

'I don't know that either!' Sir Hopsalot said.

The princess's voice floated up from deep in the well.

'When my father was a child he was given a large golden egg by a wise old wizard. The egg grants the power of life to the owner. My father decided to take the egg and use his life power to do good all across the kingdom. When my mother passed away, and my father was mourning, Wizard Greesgate stole the egg by some mean and crafty trick and he plans to destroy this kingdom once he's taken me as his bride!'

'So, what do we do?' Bobby asked.

'The egg must be destroyed!' said Sir Hopsalot.

'The trouble is, the egg is in the highest tower in the castle,' said the princess. 'It's guarded by two enormous trolls called Bubble and Squeak. No one can get past them.'

'Why?' asked Noel.

'Because they smell so bad that anyone who gets close passes out,' the princess said. 'They're also  very strong and the meanest, grumpiest trolls ever. Their favourite hobby is smashing heads together and seeing who can make the worst smell.'

'Well, I have a plan,' said Sir Hopsalot. 'And because it's my plan and because Bobby is here—'

'And me!' Noel said.

'Yes, and you,' said Sir Hopsalot. 'Because it's my plan and because Bobby and Noel are here, we will succeed, my princess! Hurrah! Now follow me!'

Sir Hopsalot bounded off towards the castle and once again Bobby and Noel had to chase after him.

Inside the castle, Bobby and Noel stood behind Sir Hopsalot at the bottom of the tallest tower.

'About this plan, then,' said Bobby.

'I'm hoping you have one,' said Sir Hopsalot.

'But you said YOU had one!' said Noel.

'I got carried away,' said Sir Hopsalot.

Bobby thought for a moment. 'We need a distraction,' he said. 'For the trolls.'

'What about the smell?' asked Sir Hopsalot.

'If we can cause a distraction and have them leave the tower, the smell won't be a problem.'

'Then leave that to me!'

Sir Hopsalot disappeared into the tower through a large open door.

'I like him,' said Noel. 'But he's very excitable.'

A roar from the tower boomed out and Bobby and Noel tumbled to the ground.

'What was that?' Noel asked.

The answer came from the door as Sir Hopsalot bounded out, chased by two huge trolls.

'Well done, Sir Hopsalot,' Bobby said, and with Noel in his pocket, charged up the tower.

At the top of the tower they found the room with the egg. It was huge and golden and looked far too big to carry back outside.

'We need to destroy it,' Bobby said. 'But how?'

Noel said, 'I wish I was as strong as those stinky trolls . . .

'Now there's an idea!' Bobby said and before Noel could stop him, he started to sing.

> *Trolls are stinky, trolls are dim.*
> *They can't do much of anything!*
> *They can't fight and they can't run*
> *And they smell like something's*
> *died in their bum!*

'Bobby! That's SO rude!' cried Noel.

A roar from the bottom of the tower rolled up to Bobby and Noel.

'Here they come!' said Bobby.

'I hope you know what you're doing!' said Noel.

The thunderous footsteps of the trolls charging up the stairs shook the tower. The two huge creatures charged into the room.

'Hold your nose, Noel!' Bobby said.

The trolls roared. 'Who called us stinky? Who was it? We don't stink! We smell of roses and lovely stuff!'

'I did!' shouted Bobby from behind the egg. 'What are you going to do about it?'

'We're going to crush you to dust!' the trolls shouted. 'Then we're going to use that dust to make pancakes and push the pancakes into our lovely faces!'

Bobby blew a raspberry.

The trolls charged.

And the egg went flying out of a tower window and smashed to pieces on the ground below.

'Oh no!' the trolls cried. 'We're for it now! Run! Run! Run!'

The tower shook once again as the trolls ran away and were never seen by anybody in the kingdom ever again.

Back down at the bottom of the tower, Bobby and Noel found Sir Hopsalot standing with an old man and a young woman.

'Bravo, Bobby!' Sir Hopsalot cheered. 'You destroyed the egg, freeing the king and the princess!'

'What about Wizard Greesgate?' Bobby asked. 'Where is he? We've not seen him yet. Has he escaped?'

'He turned to grit and dust as soon as the egg was destroyed!' the king said. 'Might use it on the castle paths when it gets icy in winter. Now, how would you like a reward?'

'Is it cheese?' asked Noel.

The king held out a tiny, smooth, golden egg for Bobby.

'Keep this close and it may help you in the future!'

Bobby clasped the egg in his hands and looked as his arm began to dissolve in front of him, then the king, princess and Sir Hopsalot disappeared. Noel ran up Bobby's leg lightning fast and went into Bobby's pocket. The sound of flutes and running water could be heard, and both Bobby and Noel closed their eyes.

13

Nigel

Bobby felt someone tugging at his sleeve and opened his eyes to see Flo staring at him.

'Look!' Flo said.

Behind a fence, the two boys were sprawled on the ground and sitting on top of them was the giant rabbit.

'We're sorry!' the boys cried. 'Please help us! Anyone!'

A security guard opened a door in the fence. 'Right you

two, come with me!' he said, as the rabbit bounced off and away.

'Ice creams all round, I reckon,' said Bobby, and the gang all cheered.

As everyone walked away Bobby took one final glance towards the giant rabbit.

'Thanks for saving me,' it said.

'You can talk!' said Bobby.

'Of course I can!' the rabbit said. 'Oh, and the king and his daughter say thanks, too!'

As Bobby turned to walk away, he looked again at the sign on the fence around the rabbit. In small letters at the very bottom of the sign, he spotted some words he hadn't seen before: 'Name: Nigel'.

Very carefully he slipped his fingers into

his coat pocket where he could feel the smooth, cold surface of a tiny egg.

That night, the gang gathered in the den. Tink took the register and all were present and correct.

'First on the agenda is the Egg-cellent Egg-stravaganza!' Tink announced. 'How's everyone getting along?'

'I'm so going to win!' boasted Polo.

'No way!' said Doug.

'You all know I have the best idea so stop kidding yourselves!' said Sasha.

'I reckon if Bobby and Flo sang a duet they could win it!' said Tink.

Florence was sitting on the floor feeding a tiny lump of cheese to Nippy.

'Mum has just finished the new

chocolate egg. It's bigger than the first one! She's kept it safely hidden away so my evil uncle won't smash it again. He just destroys everything he sets his eyes on!'

'Why is he like that?' asked Bobby.

'When my mum and her brother were children they didn't have much money,' said Flo. 'My grandparents were poor, but rich in love and kindness. My uncle hated the fact that they weren't rich and blamed his parents and was horrible to them. He was a jealous child and he got worse and worse as he got older.'

'Your grandparents sound lovely!' said Tink.

'It broke their hearts that they couldn't provide for their children. My mum helped in the sweet shop and had three jobs to help out, including a paper round, car washing and gardening!'

'How can your mum and uncle be so different?' asked Sasha.

To which Flo replied, 'Mum has always lived by the motto that it's what you have in your heart that's important not what you have in your bank account!'

'Great motto, that, Flo!' said Bobby.

'She sends her mum and dad money every month whereas my uncle does nothing. He doesn't even visit his parents! He loves money above everything else, even his own children!'

'Do you really think he'll destroy our little village?' asked Bobby.

'He does anything he wants and if he thinks it'll upset mum then he'll be happy to smash it all!'

'Then we have to try and stop him!' said Bobby. 'I just don't know how at the moment! Let's all have a think and report back here tomorrow night. All those in favour say aye!'

Everyone in the gang replied, 'Aye!'

'Just before you all go, there's someone I'd like you to finally meet. He's been my friend for a while but it's never seemed the right time to introduce him,' said Bobby. He reached into his jacket pocket and brought Noel out.

'This is Noel. He's been dying to meet you all for ages.'

'Oh, he's so cute!' said Tink.

'Adorable!' added Sasha.

'Cool mouse!' said Polo.

'And a mouse mate for Nippy!' said Doug.

As the gang started packing up their belongings Bobby noticed that Noel and Nippy were in the corner of the den, deep in conversation. They were rubbing noses!

PEN

14

The Bad News

B obby stared at the note in front of him.
Sasha had pushed it into his hands at lunch.
URGENT DEN MEETING TONIGHT AFTER DINNER!
EVERYONE MUST BE THERE! He'd
asked the rest of the gang what it
was about but no one had a clue.

'She's being really secretive,'
Doug said with a shrug.

That evening, after an enormous meal of toad in
the hole, Bobby made his way over to the den.

'Nice of you to join us!' said Doug 'Closest one to the den, last one to arrive!'

'Mum's dinner took ages,' Bobby said. 'I'm so full!'

Sasha stood up, her face serious. 'As you all know, I've been doing my mile-a-day runs all term. And I've seen stuff.'

'What stuff?' Polo asked.

'Lorries arriving in the village car park,' said Sasha. 'And yesterday a convoy of earthmovers drove in.'

'So, what's happening?' asked Polo.

'I sneaked up behind a truck where I heard two drivers chatting.'

'What did they say?' asked Bobby.

'It's not good!' replied Sasha. 'Flo's uncle is going to destroy the whole village. They're starting in the old car park tonight and then every night they'll move closer and closer to our school. He wants the school knocked down by the end of next week!'

'Are you sure you heard right?' asked Tink.

'He's going to turn the whole village into a leisure park, where people can come and pretend they live in the country for a day! There will be rollercoasters

with tractors on them, a bowling alley of milk churns, loads of fast food – and Bobby, your farm will be a huge car park!'

'What are we going to do?' asked Flo.

'We can't just sit back and let this happen,' said Tink.

'No, we can't,' said Bobby. 'We're going to have to do something.'

The next morning Mr Morris had called the whole school to the assembly hall.

'Wonder what all this is about?' asked Doug.

'Maybe he knows about "you know what"' said Sasha.

'Or it could be another day out?' said Polo hopefully. 'Or hotdogs for lunch?!'

'That's hardly important news!' said Tink.

'It is for me!' said Polo.

As Mr Morris walked onto stage, Flo grabbed onto Bobby's arm. Bobby gave her a smile and held onto her hand.

'It's going to be OK!' he whispered. Although deep down he wasn't sure it was going to be.

Everyone in the hall was silent and Mr Morris up on the stage looked as white as a restaurant tablecloth. His hair was sticking up and his suit was creased badly.

'I've never seen him like this,' said a worried Tink.

'It's like he hasn't slept all night!' said Polo.

The Bad News

'Can I please have everyone's attention!' Mr Morris's voice echoed around the hall. 'I'm sorry to have to tell you that this school might have to be knocked down!'

'Told you!' said Sasha.

There were gasps in the hall and some of the younger children started to cry.

Mr Morris went on to tell everyone exactly what Sasha had told the gang in the den the night before.

'Please don't be upset,' the head teacher continued. 'We haven't lost the fight yet and I will do everything in my power to save the school!'

'And we'll join you!' shouted Bobby.

Everyone cheered.

Mr Morris lifted his arms to quieten everyone down.

'This little setback means I have further bad news, I'm afraid!'

The hall fell deadly silent once again.

'The Egg-cellent Egg-stravaganza will have to be cancelled.'

The hall erupted with shouts of 'Oh no!' 'I really wanted that huge egg!'

Once again Mr Morris quietened everyone down.

'Thank you for your understanding. I have a letter for you all to take home to your parents at the end of the day. Please collect them from Miss Evans.

And finally, let's hope and pray that we will have a school to hold an Egg-cellent Egg-stravaganza in the future! Now off to class everyone!'

And with that he walked off stage.

'I guess my mum will have to hold on to the chocolate egg a little longer?' said Flo

'There is NO way your uncle is knocking down my village! And we WILL have our show!' said Tink.

And with that Bobby and the gang made their way to class.

15

Hot Chocolate at the Den

O n the journey home, Legin was doing his best to cheer everyone up.

'Mr D'Vine, he's just a dope! You're the kids who'll give us hope!'

No one joined in though, not even Bobby. He sat quietly looking out of the bus window, feeling the tiny, cool, golden egg in his pocket – how could he even begin to make a difference?

When he got home, Bobby found his parents sitting at the kitchen table.

'We've some bad news, Bobby,' said his dad.

Bobby sat down.

'It's the farm,' said his mum. 'There's a developer and—'

'I know all about that,' said Bobby. 'And it's not just the farm, it's the entire village, including school!'

'Miss D'Vine's brother is trying to destroy everything,' said Bobby's dad.

'It's not just about us,' said Bobby's mum. 'The farm is home to the horses and chickens and pigs too. Then there're all the different insects and wild animals that live here.'

'And what about all the plants and trees?' said Bobby's dad.

'We have to stop him!' shouted Bobby.

It was all too much for his dad and he got up and left

the kitchen. 'I'm going to check on the chickens!' he said as he closed the door behind him.

'I'll come with you,' said Bobby's mum.

Ruffian plonked his head into Bobby's lap. Noel popped out from underneath one of the dog's ears.

That evening, Bobby, Ruffian and Noel were first into the den.

'I've never seen Mum and Dad so worried,' said Bobby, as everyone sat around eating some biscuits his dad had made.

'My mum cried at dinner,' said Polo.

'The local shop owners are terrified,' said Sasha. My nan was at the hairdresser's today and they reckon they'll get knocked down next week, too!'

A loud knock at the den door broke the conversation and in came Flo.

'Sorry I'm late,' she said, 'but Mum insisted I bring this to cheer us up!'

Flo placed a bag on the floor and pulled out a large flask and mugs.

'Is that what I think it is?' Polo asked.

'Hot chocolate!' said Flo. 'And the best you've ever tasted!'

Drinks poured, Tink said, 'Right then, so how are we going to save our lovely village?'

'Flo, could you speak to your uncle?' asked Doug. 'Maybe he'll listen to you.'

'He doesn't listen to anyone,' said Flo.

'What about forming a barricade near the
trucks!' said Polo. 'We could even lie down on the road!'

Everyone agreed that was a bit extreme.

Bobby went to speak but then heard something far off.

'What's that?' he said.

Everyone stopped talking. And listened.

There was a rumbling sound outside the den, getting louder by the second.

Bobby leapt up and burst out of the den, followed by the rest of the gang.

'It can't be . . .' Doug said.

'It is,' said Bobby.

Trundling down the lane to the farm was what looked like a convoy of bulldozers and diggers.

Bobby Dean opened his mouth to yell 'stop' but instead out came a huge 'aah' and he began to sing more loudly than he'd ever done. Before he could do anything to stop it, the world around him dissolved and once more he was flying past the stars and on towards the swirling blob of colours.

16

Travelling in Time

When Bobby Dean opened his eyes, the first thing he saw was a crowd of people shouting and yelling. They were all so angry, but he could see that they were sad as well. Then he realised that he recognised them. These were the people from the village and they were marching down the road towards the bulldozers.

'What's going on, Noel?' Bobby wondered. 'Is this now? It can't be, can it?'

Then Bobby saw the gang. They all had placards and were joining in with the chants. Doug was waving a huge banner with 'Hands off our village!' scrawled on it. Polo was shouting through a megaphone about how the best thing Mr D'Vine could do would be to throw himself into a hole.

'All my friends look so different and so angry!' said Bobby.

Flo had Nippy standing on her head and even the mouse had a banner that just read 'YOU'RE A RAT, MR D'VINE!'

'Look!' Bobby said and pointed to a band who were playing at the front of the angry crowd. 'That's Legin and his reggae band!'

Bobby Dean and the Golden Egg

You're a rat Mr. D'Vine
You're a nasty little swine
You stole our village! But only for a time
'Cos things will change, Oh Mr. D'Vine

The trees and ponds for now have gone
But all that's good won't be undone
The roots below will reach for the sun
And one day the power of life will have won!

Bobby had never heard Legin sing anything with such heart and soul. He looked towards Mr D'Vine and he seemed oblivious to the villagers. He was clinking his champagne glass with someone in a suit and laughing as if he didn't have a care in the world. And then Bobby was stopped in his tracks.

'It's Mum and Dad!'

'And there's Ruff!' shouted Noel. 'Why's he just lying there with his paws over his eyes?'

'I don't think he can bear to watch,' said Bobby.

Far off, something caught Bobby's eye.

'Look,' he said, pointing to something towering over the village. 'A rollercoaster!'

'Isn't that where the school should be?' Noel said.

Bobby noticed that the trees and the pond where the gang liked to watch tadpoles turn into frogs had been replaced with concrete. All the green spaces had gone except for one square which was covered in picnic tables. Some of the village had been preserved as a museum, and dotted around everywhere were amusement arcades and fast food outlets. Above the main entrance was a banner saying, 'Grand Opening of the Perfectly Preserved Village'!

'This is horrible,' said Noel.

172

Bobby saw television cameras dotted everywhere. People in very expensive clothes were walking on a red carpet. Camera flashes were going off, here, there and everywhere.

'Is that Mr Morris?!' asked Bobby.

Both he and Noel looked towards a car that was parked by the rollercoaster. In it was Miss Evans and her young daughter. Mr Morris stood by the car.

'Why's Mr Morris crying?' asked Noel.

173

They listened in on the conversation.

'I'd better get going. I have a six-hour drive to my new school job and my little daughter hates long car journeys! I'll miss you, Mr Morris!'

'I'll miss you too, Miss Evans,' cried Mr Morris as the car pulled away.

Bobby had seen enough. He scooped up Noel and they both ran towards where Mr D'Vine was standing. They were stopped just before they reached him by two enormous security guards.

'And where do you think you're going?'

'I need to speak with Mr D'Vine!' said Bobby.

'No one speaks to the boss uninvited!' said the other security guard.

The mean developer had witnessed what was happening.

'Let the boy through! I can't wait to hear what the poor thing has to say!'

Bobby ran up to Mr D'Vine.

'You might be rich but money can't buy you happiness!'

Mr D'Vine laughed in Bobby's face. 'You watch how my money makes me smile right now!' he said as he walked up to the podium to give his speech to open the theme park.

Bobby felt a small movement in his pocket. He thought it was Noel but he was standing in his hand watching Mr D'Vine, shouting angrily. Bobby reached inside his pocket and felt the tiny, cool egg buzzing faster and faster. Just then a huge flash went off that made everything disappear!

17

Travelling in Time – again!

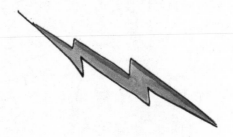

Bobby opened his eyes as a thunderclap broke the night in two. The sky lit up with a brilliant white flash, as rain hammered down into the earth.

'What just happened?' Bobby asked.

'No idea,' said Noel, crawling out of Bobby's jacket. 'But I think we've travelled in time again. Look!'

Noel pointed to a neon sign that read 'The Perfectly Preserved Village Experience'. It was swinging vertically by one end and flashing on and off. Three of the letters weren't lit at all. Gone were the crowds and the glitz and glamour of television and newspaper cameras. There was total stillness.

'Everything is derelict!' said Bobby, 'The rollercoaster has even broken in two!'

Next to it one of the rollercoaster cars sat covered in rust. All the bright canopies were ripped and the colours looked faded and dirty.

'This is so spooky!' said Noel.

'Like a scene from a horror film!' said Bobby.

'Wonder what happened here?' asked Noel.

'Let's ask him!' said Bobby, pointing to a lone man who was sitting on the curb side.

As he approached the man Bobby saw that he had

his head in his hands. He was dressed in rags and his shoes had holes in them, and he was soaked through to the bone. The man slowly lifted his head and looked at Bobby. It was Mr D'Vine, the developer.

'What happened?' asked Bobby.

'No one came to the theme park, is what happened!' said Mr D'Vine. 'I've lost everything! My money, yes, but most importantly, my family. My greed drove them away! And now I have no one and nothing!'

Bobby was silent and just let the man talk. As he listened, Bobby wrapped his fingers around the tiny, cool, golden egg in his pocket. It was beginning to buzz again.

'I let my love of money and my stupid anger at my parents and sister ruin everything.'

'Maybe it's not too late,' said Bobby. He took hold of Mr D'Vine's hand and led him into the village.

'Look!' said Bobby, pointing to where the tarmac under their feet had cracked open. 'Little tree shoots are growing again! And look at the beautiful flowers blooming by the side of the road!'

'I remember a song about that,' said the developer. 'Something about nature and the power of life always winning the battle.'

'Why don't you focus on building something amazing instead of always destroying things?' said Bobby. 'I'm sure it would make you happier!'

The tiny, golden egg in Bobby's pocket was buzzing so much it was almost jumping around. Just then Bobby remembered what the king had said when he'd given it to Bobby It has the power to make things live . . . Bobby took the egg and carefully placed it into the crack in the tarmac. It disappeared into the soil with a glug.

'Please,' prayed Bobby, 'please make things the way they were.'

He turned around to see that the developer has stopped a few feet back. He was looking over Bobby's head – two people were coming their way.

Coco D'Vine and Flo were walking towards Bobby and Mr D'Vine.

Bobby and Noel watched as brother and sister embraced.

'I'm so sorry for everything,' said Mr D'Vine. 'I want to make amazing things and not destroy them. And Florence? I can't offer you the money I once had but I want to be the best uncle ever! I will open my heart and give you love!'

'Why don't you join forces and create something special together?' said Bobby.

Bobby Dean and Noel watched the three D'Vines hugging, and suddenly his body started to tingle. Noel darted up Bobby's leg and into his trouser pocket, just in time for the world around them to start to blur and spin.

And with that Bobby was twisting and turning and being sucked back to his real life.

18

The Egg-cellent Egg-stravaganza!

Bobby and Noel arrived back in the den with all the gang around them, but the rumbling sound was louder than ever. It was almost deafening.

'Brace for impact!' said Doug and the gang huddled together.

The door to the den opened.

'Dad?' said Sasha.

'HELLO, LOVE!' said a man in the doorway. 'YOU READY?'

'Why are you shouting?' Sasha asked.

'SHOUTING? I'M NOT SHOUTING!'

'Yes, you are!' Sasha said.

The man looked confused then said, 'Is this better?'

'Yes,' Sasha said with a nod.

'Sorry,' said her dad. 'The exhaust dropped off the car on the way over. Think I've gone a bit deaf!'

Sasha headed off with her dad.

'Hey Bobby, I had an idea . . .' said Flo. 'Maybe we should sing it as a duet if the Egg-cellent Egg-stravaganza ever happens.'

'It will definitely happen!' said Bobby.

'What makes you so sure?' asked Polo.

'Just call it a hunch!' said Bobby, as he remembered the events of his last adventure.

'Right! Same time tomorrow night, OK?' said Tink. 'We must come up with a plan to stop that ruthless developer!'

The next morning Mr Morris's voice came out loud and clear from the classroom speaker. 'Could the whole school gather in the assembly hall immediately!'

'That nearly gave me a heart attack!' said Sasha.

'Wonder what all that's about?' said Tink. 'And if you say hotdogs, I swear I'll tickle you to death!' she added, looking towards Polo.

'Maybe it's another announcement about the school,' said Doug. 'I'm dreading that!'

'Or the Egg-cellent Egg-stravaganza is cancelled forever!' said Polo.

'Maybe it's good news!' said Bobby.

'Ever the optimist!' said Tink. 'Let's hope you're right this time!'

Everyone made their way to the hall. Unusually, they all sat there in silence.

'Good morning, everyone!' said Mr Morris as he walked onto the stage.

'Good morning, Mr Morris!' replied the school.

'I'd like you to meet someone very special. Please welcome Mr D'Vine!'

The developer walked onto the stage to stunned silence.

'Has Mr Morris lost his mind?' whispered Tink.

'This cannot be good!' said Sasha.

'Good morning, everyone!' said Mr D'Vine.

The hall remained silent. All eyes sent daggers the developer's way.

'First, I'd like to apologise to you all. I'm aware I've given you some sleepless nights. I have seen the error of my ways. The good news is I am not going to turn the school and the village into a theme park!'

The hall erupted with loud cheers.

'I still don't trust him!' whispered Tink to Bobby.

'Instead, I intend to use my money to create nature reserves here and all over the world. And I will be creating a special project planting cacao trees with my dear sister Coco and her daughter Flo. Please welcome Miss D'Vine to the stage.'

On walked Coco D'Vine, carrying a small cacao tree in a beautiful pot. ' I can almost smell the chocolate already!' she said.

The hall erupted once again with even more applause and cheers. Even Tink whooped with delight.

Coco D'Vine began to speak.

'My brother and I have decided that this school deserves something special by way of apology. So we will be building a brand new adventure playground for you all and a very special garden where you can grow your own food!'

The cheers were so loud, Bobby thought they were going to raise the roof off the school!

'And there is another apology that needs to be made,' said Mr D'Vine, 'Will Bobby Dean please come up to the stage.'

Bobby was shocked but stood up and made his way to the platform.

'For too long, a member of this village has been blamed for something they did not do.' Mr D'Vine continued, 'I want to publicly clear his name and acknowledge his good character, his bravery and keen eye for justice.'

'Mr Morris, my sister and I would like to introduce you to this excellent role model in the community and the mascot for a brand new business we're creating. Please put your hands together for Mr and Mrs Dean and Ruffian the dog!'

Ruffian bounded onto the stage – the electronic tag was gone and in its place was a shiny new collar with a small golden medal.

Bobby was totally confused by what was happening.

Mr D'Vine went to hand Ruffian something.

'Stop!' shouted Bobby. 'Dogs shouldn't eat chocolate!'

'Don't worry, Bobby!' said Miss D'Vine. 'It's not chocolate, it's a Ruffian Rusk! Our new project is special treats for dogs. Everyone, meet Ruffian, our mascot!'

Ruffian's tail wagged wildly and he licked Mr D'Vine's hand.

Once again there were loud cheers and whoops.

Bobby gave Ruffian a cuddle, and spotted Noel hiding under Ruff's ear. They winked at one another. Mum and Dad came over and gave Bobby a cuddle too.

Mr Morris stepped up to the platform.

'This is wonderful news! And thanks to the D'Vines for creating something that will be enjoyed by this community for ever. All that's left for me to announce is BRING ON THE EGG-CELLENT EGG-STRAVAGANZA!'

Everyone in the hall stood up and jumped around. There was an explosion of happy sounds!

For Bobby it had been the best day of his life. The school had come alive with music and dancing. Mr and Miss D'Vine had declared everyone the winners of the competition and had broken up the new giant chocolate egg for the whole school to share.

'I think the news of the development has spread,' announced Mr Morris, 'and we have a bigger party to join in the village!'

Everyone stepped outside to the reggae sounds of Legin and his band. Bobby and the gang were amazed by what they saw. There were food stalls and fairground arcades dotted around. And a massive musical parade formed that passed through the whole village, as the entire community joined in with the singing and partying.

The gang gathered together.

'I can't believe all this is happening!' shouted Doug, over the music.

'It's a miracle!' said Tink!

'I've never seen everyone so happy!' said Sasha.

'And I've already had my first hotdog! said
Polo.

Everyone laughed and ran to the food
stall.

Bobby watched as his gang, his
best friend Ruffian and his family
enjoyed the party and his heart was
full of joy. He sighed to himself.
Then he caught a glimpse of a
golden glint in one of the trees near
the side of the stage. On it was the tiniest bunch of
smooth, little golden eggs, just budding from the
plant. He smiled knowing that he had something to
turn to if things got out of hand in the future.
Before he could think much more about them,

another thing caught his eye: there by the keyboard on stage Bobby spotted Noel and Nippy dancing arm in arm.

Flo walked up to Bobby.

'I was worried when another mouse joined the gang, but I'm so glad they are getting on well,' she said.

Bobby laughed.

'Noel needed another mouse friend. And I think they'll be friends for life! Just like us! Right – are you ready for our duet?'

Bobby noticed that Flo looked a little nervous.

'Something wrong?' he asked.

'It's just that singing is your thing, isn't it?' said Flo.

'Of course it isn't!' said Bobby. 'Singing is everyone's thing!

Flo's frown turned to a huge smile.

'You ready?' Bobby asked.

'You bet!' Flo said.

'Then let's do this!' Bobby cheered and ran onto stage, Flo at his side.

Go on more adventures with Bobby Dean!

Go back to Bobby's first term at school . . .

OUT NOW | 9781529376128

Coming soon . . .

Bobby Dean and
the Underground Kingdom

SUMMER 2022 | 9781529383195